My Friend's Got This Problem, Mr. Candler

My Friend's Got This Problem, Mr. Candler

High School Poems
by Mel Glenn

Photographs by
Michael J. Bernstein

Clarion Books
New York

For Elyse, again

and

For the staff and students of Lincoln High School

Clarion Books
a Houghton Mifflin Company imprint
215 Park Avenue South, New York, NY 10003
Text copyright © 1991 by Mel Glenn
Photographs copyright © 1991 by Michael J. Bernstein
All rights reserved.
For information about permission to reproduce
selections from this book, write to Permissions,
Houghton Mifflin Company, 2 Park Street, Boston, MA 02108.
Printed in U.S.A.

Library of Congress Cataloging-in-Publication Data
Glenn, Mel.
    My friend's got this problem, Mr. Candler / by Mel Glenn ;
photographs by Michael Bernstein.
        p.   cm.
Summary: Fourth in a series of photo-illustrated poetry
collections, this one centers on the high school guidance counselor
and the variety of students and parents he encounters during the
week.
    ISBN 0–89919–833–3
    1. Young adult poetry, American. 2. High school students—Poetry.
3. High schools—Poetry. [1. High schools—Poetry, 2. Schools—
Poetry. 3. American poetry.] I. Bernstein, Michael J., ill.
II. Title.
PS3557.L447M9 1991
811'.54—dc20   90–1414
                                                       CIP
                                                       AC

HAL 10 9 8 7 6 5 4 3 2 1

Contents

MONDAY

TUESDAY

WEDNESDAY

THURSDAY

FRIDAY

Author's Note

The characters in this book are fictional
composites of the many students I have
taught through the years. Maureen, Stefan,
Madeline, and all the others live on
these pages, not in real life. Yet any
resemblance to actual persons is purely
intentional in the artistic sense.

MONDAY

Jennifer Leeds

"You go in, I'll wait out here."
   "No way, Jen, he'll kill me."
"If he doesn't, I will."
   "But I haven't been to school in a week."
"Nobody missed you, 'cept me."
   "You're funny."
"I know."
   "My parents are gonna murder me."
"I know. That's why you gotta talk to him."
   "I don't need a counselor."
"Joey!"
   "I'll come back tomorrow,
      let's go grab breakfast."
"You split now and it's over between us."
   "Come on, Jen, get serious."
"I mean it, Joey. Just knock on the door."
   "I don't know what to say to him."
"What we talked about. Just ask him."
   "OK."
"I'll be here waitin' for you, Joey,
Like always."

Joey Foster

Mr. Candler, got a minute?
Finish your coffee, I can come back.
OK, I'll sit, but only for a minute.
Yeah, I heard you were looking for me.
From Jennifer, Jennifer Leeds.
She *is* nice.
My parents are worried about me?
Then why did they throw me out?
Well, I still ain't goin' home,
Not for a while at least.
Stayin' with a friend.
The thing of it is, Mr. C.,
Could you call up my folks,
Tell 'em I'm all right
And see if they'll speak to me?
I don't know which I can't stand more,
Me not talking to them
Or them not talking to me.

Mr. Lloyd Foster

(Joey's father) • Telephone conversation

Mr. Candler? I'd like to sign my son
    out of school.
How do I go about it?
Actually, it's the last thing I want to do.
But Joey's left me no choice.
   He hangs out with his friends.
   He drives his car all hours.
   He's not even livin' at home now.
   He's with that girl, whatshername.
Of course I don't like it!
I tell him,
"Joey, you want to fry burgers your whole life?
You want to collect unemployment?"
But he doesn't listen to me anymore.
He thinks he knows it all.
Let him see how tough the real world is. . . .
How do I sign him out?

Walter Finney

Hi, Mr. Candler, how ya doin'?
Not much. What about you?
My weekend? Not too bad.
My mom dragged me to a shrink.
He said I was "manic depressive,"
Whatever that means.
I thought I was just sad.
What about? Things.
Like? I got no girlfriend.
Everybody treats me bad.
And I'm ugly—you need more?
Don't give me that garbage
About things gettin' better,
'Cause they won't.
My heart just aches all the time.
How's a shrink gonna fix that?

Maureen McDermott

Yo, Mr. Candler,
'Scuse the interruption.
I just gotta tell you.
I passed Pettis's history exam.
Outrageous!
There was too much to study—
All his notes,
All those pages,
All the homeworks.
Pettis is so mean
He eats students for breakfast,
But I respect him a lot.
He made me love history.
I never knew dead people could be so lively.
I'm never going to forget
What he did for me.
Did you see my brother?
I wonder what he got.
Me? A 92.
Isn't that just great?

Hugh McDermott

Yo, Mr. Candler,
'Scuse the interruption.
I just gotta tell you
I failed Pettis's history exam.
Outrageous!
There was too much to study—
All his notes,
All those pages,
All the homeworks.
Pettis is so mean
He eats students for breakfast,
And I despise him a lot.
He made me hate history.
I never knew dead people could be so deadly.
I'm never going to forget
What he did to me.
Did you see my sister?
I wonder what she got.
Me? A 29.
Isn't that just great?

Miki London

Oh, you caught me.
Mr. Candler, please let me practice here in
    the hall.
I'm so nervous I could die.
Twirler tryouts are today,
And if I don't make the team
I'm gonna move to another city.
I know I shouldn't think so negatively,
But you don't know what it's like
To have your whole social future,
The right parties, the right guys,
Depending on a two-minute routine.
All those eyes staring at you,
Criticizing your every move,
It's enough to drive you insane.
It all comes down to
A simple twist of the wrist,
A simple twist of fate.
Please, God, don't let me drop my baton.
I promise I'll be good the rest of my life.

Ivy Hayden

Mr. Candler, I can't take it anymore.
My mother hits me,
A lot more than she used to.
She'll be all right for a couple of weeks or so
And then something'll set her off
And she'll start to swing wildly at me.
I just cover my head and wait for her to stop.
I want so much to hit her back,
But I can't; she's my mother.
At night before I finally fall asleep
I try to think if I did something
To make her act crazy like that.
I swear to God I don't do anything,
Anything, anything!
Please Mr. Candler, help me.
She can't help herself, she's sick.
And I don't think I can take it
Anymore!

Felicia Goodwin

I can't talk to my parents about sex!
They get so embarrassed.
My girlfriends think I'm an absolute prude
Because I don't go to wild parties with them.
But I think sex is a sacred thing, don't you?
The problem is that my boyfriend
Is going away to boot camp and
He wants to, you know.
I know I'm not ready.
Sex is not a going-away present.
But if I don't, he will, with someone else.
I thought if people loved each over
They would want to wait for each other.
Don't people wait for each other anymore?
I keep thinking love is more than sex.
I guess my boyfriend thinks
It's the other way around.

Terrance Kane

Mr. Candler, you busy?
Listen, I got this serious problem.
I'm really hurtin' and I don't know who
    to talk to.
I can't tell any of the guys on the team.
It's about Cindy, Cindy Lucas.
She comes over to me the other day and says,
"Terry, you're not going to like this,
But I think we should see other people."
"I only want to see you," I say.
"No good," she says. "I'm going away to
    school soon
And I want to feel free, so here's your
    ring back."
Just like that—a three-month relationship
    down the tubes.
Please don't tell me there are other fish in
    the sea.
Cindy is the only one I want to catch.
I can't think straight or do anything.
When does the pain go away, Mr. Candler?
When does it go away?

Norma Testerman

How do I know where I'll go?
        Live home or away,
        Big school or small,
        East or West?
How do I know what I'll like?
        Dorm or off-campus,
        Roommate or single,
        Cafeteria or restaurant?
How do I know what I'll do?
        Bio major or English,
        Full time or part time,
        Grad school or business?
How do I know if I'll succeed?
        What if I make a mistake?
        What if I fail my courses?
        What if people don't like me?
I thought college would provide answers,
Not a whole bunch of new questions.
. . . Er, Mr. Candler, would you fill out
This recommendation for me, please?

Patrick DeShannon

My little brother, Brendan, is a pain.
He never leaves me alone.
He always messes up my room,
Looking for my magazines, he says.
He makes horrible bird noises,
Which embarrasses me in front of my friends.
And when I scream at him,
Calling him all sorts of names,
He goes running to my mother,
Who says, "Stop teasing him, you're older."
I tell him to get lost,
But he follows me everywhere.
"He wants to be like you," my mother says.
Last week, in order to get Brendan off my back,
I taught him how to ride my bike.
It took the little pain three days to learn.
Now he rides everywhere with *his* friends.
I miss him.

Mrs. Judith Goodwin

(Felicia's mother) • Telephone conversation

I don't want my daughter
Learning about sex in school.
My daughter, Felicia, is a good girl,
But I saw her hygiene book the other day
And I couldn't believe the pictures I saw.
Such filth.
Bad enough there is so much sex
In the movies and on TV.
I can control what Felicia learns at home.
I am horrified to find out
What she learns in school.
If my daughter is going to learn about sex,
Let her learn naturally and properly—
After she's married.

TUESDAY

Pablo Negron

Hey, mornin', Mr. C.
How's it goin'?
Sun's shining and no rain
And I got no tests today.
Two yesterday, though—did OK, I think.
I'm in a great mood.
Am I on somethin'?
You crazy, man? No way.
Just jogged a couple of miles around the track.
You should try it.
You poisoning your body with all that
        caffeine junk.
Trouble with you is
You just sit around and hear stories all day.
What's happenin' in your own life?
OK, OK, I'm goin', see ya soon.
And get rid of that coffee.
It's bad for you, man.

Earl Fiske, Jr.

I look a bit green?
Well, I'm still recovering from
       my weekend, Mr. C.
Man, it was a blast.
Me and some of the guys went drinking
       and . . . what?
Fake ID's, you can get 'em easy.
We were tossing back a few beers,
Then a few more,
And a few more after that.
I stopped counting 'em after a while.
I stopped seeing 'em after a while, too.
Then everything became kinda fuzzy.
I got sick to my stomach
And spent my seventeenth birthday in
       Flanagan's Bar and Grill,
In the toilet.
Man, I had a real great time.
I can't wait for this weekend.

Cora Galloway

What with work and all
I know my grades haven't been up to par.
Yeah, I work every day after school in
    a card store.
Five hours a day, thought you knew about it.
When I come home I'm too tired to do
    any homework.
No, I don't think I can cut down on my hours.
I need the money.
The job's OK, but there is one little problem—
The boss.
He doesn't yell at me or anything;
    on the contrary,
He's *too* nice, if you know what I mean.
He's always touching me,
You know, my hand, my shoulder, my waist.
I know what's on his mind.
No, I can't say anything.
He'd get someone new in a second,
And I need the money, like I told you.
Mr. Candler, don't worry.
I can keep him off me till I graduate.
Let me ask you something, though.
Is the real business world like this?

Mr. Earl Fiske, Sr.

(Earl Jr.'s father) • Telephone conversation

You're kidding. He failed three subjects?
Wait till I get ahold of him next weekend.
That's right, I only see him on weekends now.
Divorced—about three months.
What do you mean that's when his marks
    started going down?
You tellin' me he's goofin' off because
Me and his mother split up?
No way I buy that.
He's just lazy, that's all.
Always has been.
His mother lets him get away with murder.
But that's gonna stop, here and now.
I'll talk to him this weekend, you bet.
His grades'll get better.
Or else.
Or else what?
Or else I'll drag his mother back to court
So fast her head will swim.

Mrs. Lenore Galloway

(Cora's mother) • Telephone conversation

Yes, I'd like to speak to someone in charge.
To whom am I speaking?
Mr. Candler? Perhaps you could help me, sir.
There seems to be some error.
I received a card in the mail
Stating that my daughter, Cora,
Has been late to school thirteen times
        this month.
Why, that's simply absurd!
My daughter would never do such a thing.
Clearly your computer is at fault.
I'm sure Cora leaves for school
Right after I leave for work.
No, I do not have the time to come up to school.
I'm simply too busy in the office this time
        of year.
Please see to it that this mistake is
        taken care of.
We wouldn't want a silly oversight on your part
To be on her record, would we?
Thank you so much for your time and trouble.

Wayne Buford

You eatin' lunch early today, Mr. C.?
Brown baggin' it, I see. Mind if I join you?
Me, I got peanut butter again.
No, life ain't been too good lately.
My father just lost his job at the plant.
He's been with the company nearly thirty years
And suddenly they close the place, just like that.
Where's a fifty-five-year-old man gonna find
    another job?
It's killing him.
My mother got a job at the local Seven-Eleven.
She says the customers are crazy.
She's on her feet all day.
It's killing her.
I've been trying to find work too,
But no luck. Know of anything?
I think my family's dying by degrees.
I better get used to peanut butter.

Verna Prolinskaya

Mr. Candler, I feel my life is over.
Don't laugh, I'm serious.
I want to go to college
But my father says there's no money.
For my older brothers he had money,
But there is none left for me.
My father feels that all girls
Should stay home and wait to get married.
I tell him I want to study music.
What do you need that junk for, he says.
Yes, I know about loans.
Then I will be in debt forever.
My father promises he will help me
Find a job when I graduate,
As long as it's local.
My dreams are bigger than
A daily bus ride and a weekly check.
I feel my life is over,
At sixteen.

Sahr Amara

Mr. Candler, I have been in this country for
    six months.
Yet I do not understand much about
    American teenagers.
They have so much, but nothing of value.
They want even more, but nothing satisfies them.
In West Africa when I was in primary school
I had to walk three miles a day to school
    —barefooted.
Here if they do not have cars it is
    a technological tragedy.
In my country if I ate more than one time a day
I thanked Allah for his blessing.
Here they eat for lack of something
    better to do.
In my country education is a gift, much prized.
Here it is considered an arduous task,
    much hated.
Mind you, I am not criticizing the American teen.
He is open and friendly like the morning
    African sun,
But, alas, he is also as shallow as the stream
In the road during the rainy season.
I am trying hard to understand American culture.
It will take me more than six months.

Virginia Pilgrim

There isn't going to be any fight, Mr. C.
But she started it.
What's she yellin' at me for,
Calling me foul-mouthed names?
I don't even know the girl.
I hear she's been spreading lies 'bout me.
If you ask me, there's too many of *them* in
    this school,
Acting like they own the place.
Me?
I get along with everybody.
Yeah, yeah, get her in here.
No fight, I promise.
We can work it out.
She better watch her step, though.
Nobody starts with me.
I'll talk to her, OK?

Tamara Jackson

There ain't gonna be no fight, Mr. C.
But she started it.
What's she comin' in my face for,
Callin' me all kinds of dirt?
I don't even know the girl.
I hear she's been tellin' stories about me.
If you ask me, there's too many of *them* in
    this school,
Actin' like they own the place.
Me?
I get along with everybody.
Yeah, yeah, get her in here.
No fight, I promise.
We can work it out.
She better watch her step, though.
Hey, nobody messes with me.
I'll talk to her, OK?

Anthony Ricci

My father dreamed of football
While he worked on the boats in the bay.
My mother said when I was born
He put a football in my crib instead of
    a teddy bear.
And when he wasn't workin'
He was tossin' me a football,
    over and over again.
His love was measured in yards thrown and
    catches received.
All his life on the boats,
And what's he got to show for it?
A bad back and scarred hands
And a son who plays football for the varsity.
Well, last week I got hurt in a game.
It was a cheap shot.
The ref had blown the play dead
And then this huge Number 58 piled on me.
I heard something in my knee snap.
That linebacker ended my pro dreams,
    Mr. Candler.
He also broke my father's heart.
I'd like to go out on the boat with
    my old man, soon,
Put my arm around him and tell him
The years we spent together were not in vain.

Mr. Mack Pilgrim

(Virginia's father) • Telephone conversation

Hey, man, nobody is going to mess with
    my daughter.
I'm tellin' you that, you hear me?
If those two girls want to fight it out,
Who are you to stop it?
Don't get me wrong, I'm not tellin'
My daughter to start somethin',
But I'm not tellin' her to back off neither.
Inside school maybe you can suspend her for
    fightin',
But outside of school it's a whole 'nother
    ballgame.
I raised my daughter to fight her own battles,
Not to take crap from nobody.
If it's gonna mean a few bruises
For her to learn that,
It's more important than anything in her books.
I'll tell you one more thing.
If my Virginia don't take care of
    that other girl,
She better not come home.
I ain't raisin' no wimp, got that?

WEDNESDAY

Monroe Crawford

You Mr. Candler?
I'm supposed to speak to you.
I don't know why; registration sent me over.
Transferred officially, as of yesterday.
My school was too preppy, didn't like it much.
Everyone running around with little animals on
    their shirts.
Besides, all the teams had stupid bird names.
You know, the track team was called the Flyers,
The football team, the Ravens,
The band, the Sandpipers.
You get the picture.
What do you mean, the "real" reason?
Well, you'll find out anyway.
I got kicked out for smoking pot in the bathroom.
Hey, if they kicked out everyone who smokes
They wouldn't have half a school left.
Don't worry, I'll stay out of trouble here.
I promise.
Don't you trust me?

Stephanie Royer

Mr. Candler, you ever wonder about life?
I mean about how unfair it is.
Real life—not like what you see on TV,
Where people change partners and wardrobes
Every ten minutes or so.
I have everything I need to be happy:
My own phone, nice friends,
Parents who love me and decent grades.
But my brother Chad, who's nine and adorable,
Who is the sweetest little boy alive,
Has cancer.
The doctors think they got all of it
In his last operation, but they aren't one hundred
      percent sure.
I feel so guilty about being so lucky
When Chad isn't
That whenever I'm happy
I feel I shouldn't be.
My parents tell me that Chad's illness
Isn't physically contagious.
My parents tell me there's nothing I can do
But pray for him and love him.
I pray every night
And love him all the time,
But it isn't enough, Mr. Candler,
It just isn't enough.

Mrs. Roberta Royer

(Stephanie's mother) • Telephone conversation

It's an awkward age for my daughter.
She's too young to drive and
Too old to take my hand.
She's too young to get engaged and
Too old for puppy love.
Sometimes, when she dresses up for a party,
    you know
She looks like she's in her mid-twenties.
And sometimes, when she's just hangin' around,
Dressed in a sweatshirt and jeans,
You'd swear she was a boy.
Why am I calling?
No emergency.
I just wanted to make sure
She's all right, I mean doing all right.
You hear so many stories about kids today,
What with all the drugs, sex and violence around,
It makes you fearful about the future.
Well, thank goodness she's OK,
And thank you for your time.
I didn't mean to ramble on so.
It's an awkward age for me, too, I guess.

Perry Stubbs

My friend's got this problem, you see,
And he asked me to ask you
What he should do about it.
He got this girl kinda pregnant.
Well then, definitely pregnant.
Now the girl wants nothing to do with him,
Won't even let him know when the baby is born.
I'm askin' you, don't I, I mean he,
Have any rights to this kid?
It takes two to tango, know what I mean?
. . . Discuss it with her?
He can't find her; she's dropped out, split.
Tell his parents?
Are you serious?
They'd absolutely murder him.
For being so stupid.
Mr. Candler, why are you looking at
    me like that?
You don't think. . . .
It isn't me, Mr. Candler.
Really it isn't.
Really.

Arcadia Ross

I often go shopping with my father's
    girlfriend.
She's only a few years older than me,
And we're both the same size.
She'll call me up and tell me about
A wonderful sale on fall coats,
And I'll tell her about
A marvelous pair of shoes I saw.
We both love the same things:
Artichoke hearts, gold jewelry,
And my father.
They're going to be married soon.
I can't stand people who tell me
I'm supposed to hate her because
She's "taking away my father,"
And all that junk.
I've never seen him happier.
Mr. Candler, I don't see any problem either,
Except one.
I love Claire so much, like a sister.
I can't possibly call her "Mom."

Phillip Zavala

Mr. Candler, I ask you,
Is it too much to want a
Pretty,
Sexy,
Funny,
Reliable,
Smart (but not too smart),
Non-nerdy,
Unattached
Girl
Who is free Saturday nights
For
Movies,
Ice skating,
Dancing or
Whatever?
Don't tell me how big this school is.
There's nobody to go out with.

Connie Morrison

Mr. Candler, I ask you,
Is it too much to want a
Cute,
Sexy,
Funny,
Reliable,
Smart (but not too smart),
Non-nerdy,
Unattached
Guy
Who is free Saturday nights
For
Movies,
Ice-skating,
Dancing or
Whatever?
Don't tell me how big this school is.
There's nobody to go out with.

Lizette Ramirez

I wouldn't know love
If it stood up and smacked me in the face.
Every day in my fourth period class
A paper heart, red with scalloped edges,
Appeared taped to the corner of my desk,
With "I love you, guess who?" written in
    the middle.
No one knew who put it there,
But, boy, did I take abuse for it.
"Lizzy, you need a transplant?"
"Lizzy, how many boyfriends you got?"
"Lizzy, you tearing up another heart?"
I couldn't take it no more, so
One day I stood up and screamed:
"Will the jerk who's sendin' me hearts
Step up like a man or just shut up!"
Subtle, huh.
Well, that was the last heart I ever seen.
I must have scared him away.
You know, it's probably the best love
I ever found and lost.
I guess he didn't have the heart to stick around.

Mr. Richard Stubbs

(Perry's father) • Telephone conversation

Mr. Candler, can you talk to my son, Perry?
I can't, and I've tried.
Whenever I ask him a question
He answers, "Fine."
"How's school?"
"Fine."
"How are you feeling?"
"Fine."
"How do you feel about the end of the world?"
"Fine."
Then he barricades himself in his room
And listens to that heavy metal junk.
I can't get through to him,
Literally *and* figuratively.
Mr. Candler, I'm worried.
Can you help me talk to my own son?

Melissa Cohen

My mother called, right?
She didn't?
Well, she will—soon.
I guarantee it.
I wish she'd get off my case for a while.
I know she loves me, but come on.
If I sneeze she fills me with chicken soup.
If I cough, she immediately calls up the doctor.
If I have a fever, she acts as if I'm a
    plague victim.
And if I'm not home on time, she's ready to
    call the cops.
The other day I tried out for cheerleaders,
    right?
I was about to do my routine
And I see my mother in the stands watching me.
Everybody was asking who the old lady was.
You want to know how embarrassed I felt?
Yeah, we talk about it,
Even fight about it.
I wish she'd stop smothering me.
Mr. Candler, the more she loves me,
The more I hate her.

Edwin Sudsbury

When I saw the F on my paper,
I freaked.
When I ripped it up in little pieces,
Mr. Marshall freaked.
He said, "You don't know how to write."
I said, "You don't know how to teach."
We stared at each other,
Then I cursed him good.
That's why I'm here, isn't it?
He had no right to give me that grade.
Who does he think he is?
I did a lot of work on that paper.
I copied out of three encyclopedias.
It took me a whole day to do it.
What does he want, blood?
I tried my best.

Mrs. Rose Cohen

(Melissa's mother) • Telephone conversation

Mr. Candler, I'm Rose Cohen, Melissa's mother.
You were expecting my call?
Oh, I see.
What kind of stories has she been telling you?
That I'm mean, I hit her, child abuse, possibly?
That I go dancing in night clubs, perchance?
That I don't feed her, neglect her, perhaps?
Why shouldn't I be sarcastic?
She fights with me over everything.
You should see the boys she associates with.
You could die from them.
Space, she wants space?
If she wants space let her rent a rocket ship.
Did she tell you she gets asthma attacks?
Bad ones?
I bet she didn't tell you that.
So I bring her a little medicine sometimes,
    big crime.
Mr. Candler, do you have any children?
Then you know.
You know what a parent goes through.
Try telling *her* that.
Hah!

THURSDAY

Tara Madison

Oh, excuse me, Mr. Candler,
Sorry I spilled your coffee.
Did you see Eddie? Not yet, huh?
Yeah, I like him; oh Lord, do I like him.
He's just so sexy looking I could die.
My friends say I can't go out with him
Because I'm a senior and he's a junior.
Who cares about that?
I think I frighten him, though.
I look him straight in the eye and he turns away.
I just love guys who are shy.
Wish he'd ask me out already.
A girl can't wait forever, you know.
Maybe I'll just stop him in the hall
And give him a big wet kiss.
That ought to wake him up,
Give him an idea of what I have in mind
For us,
Alone.
Together.

Eddie Kroll

I don't know why Larkin sent me down here.
I was just readin' my paper,
    mindin' my own business
When he went crazy on me and . . .
Yeah, I'll start at the beginnin'.
Larkin was talkin' about this supply and
    demand stuff
And Zawicki yells out, "Hey, that describes
    my last date.
I got a real demand, only there's no supply."
Larkin throws him outta the room.
Then the old man starts in on me.
He comes over and rips up my newspaper
And drops it in little pieces on my head.
Even then I didn't mouth off at him.
I just told him he was deprivin' me of
    my education.
Explain? Why sure.
Economics: I read where my stocks went up.
Math: I figure the odds on a longshot.
English: I compose a personal ad for Zawicki.
Science: I glance at the weather map.
Phys. Ed.: I study the sports page.
You don't buy it either?
Well you gotta admit it's worth a shot.
Yeah, yeah, yeah, I'll go talk to Larkin.

Rodney Whitaker

My parents hold hands and hug each other.
Totally embarrassing.
Once when my friend walked into my kitchen
To get a glass of water,
He saw them kissing.
Come on, married people don't do that.
Next week they're celebrating their
        twenty-fifth anniversary.
My older sister, Sara, is throwing a party
        for them,
A party where they plan to renew their vows.
Totally mushy.
Practically all my friends are Ping-Pong balls
Bouncing from one separated parent to another,
Wearing two sets of clothes,
Depending on whose turn it is, weekend-wise.
I find myself apologizing
For having no divorce war stories,
For admitting I have parents who love each other,
For knowing they will live happily ever after.
Totally comforting.

Stefan Blumenthall

Mr. C., I just got mugged.
Outside, a block from school.
Two guys jumped me.
I was late and I was running to . . .
Yeah, I'm OK.
No, I didn't recognize them.
I don't want to report it to the police.
I don't want to tell my parents, either.
I tell them about it and they'll ground me for life.
Bad enough they don't like this school.
Bad enough they want me home way before dark
Where milk and cookies will keep me
    safe forever,
Safe from the toughs who hang out
    on the streets.
Please, Mr. Candler, I can handle it.
Really.
Five dollars is all they got, no big deal.
. . . I think I'd like to go home now,
If you don't mind.

Mr. Adolphus Whitaker

(Rodney's grandfather) • Telephone conversation

Yes, I'd like to speak to Rodney Whitaker.
I am his grandfather.
Is it an emergency? Why no, son,
It's a chronic situation with me.
Who is this? Ah, yes,
Mr. Candler, the counselor.
I wonder if you would be so kind
As to tell my grandson to call me.
I haven't heard from him in quite a while.
Tell him his granddaddy wants to hear from him,
Even though they stuck me in this place;
Tell him he can come visit me anytime he wants to
And that we can still go for walks,
Although not on trails like we used to.
You see, I've been rather dependent on my cane
        lately.
He must be fifteen now; he's such a good boy.
Oh, seventeen, you don't say.
Please reach my grandson for me,
If you would be so kind.

Dionne Sable

I couldn't wait to chuck that hick place
And come back to school here, Mr. Candler.
My mother had this weirdo idea that
She would like to be a country lawyer.
I went to the local high school there
And tried to fit in.
But I might as well have been a Martian.
They made fun of my accent, my clothes,
        everything.
Do you know that if you wear green on Thursday,
        you're horny?
I didn't know that either.
This one doofus in overalls kept following me,
Said I was the coolest thing around.
He even came to my house to ask me out.
I told my mother to tell him that I was asleep,
No matter what time he called.
"You sleep a lot," my doofus said.
"You bet," I said.
You don't know how happy I am to be home,
        Mr. Candler,
Where you can get pizza after eleven P.M.
And the sound of crickets doesn't drive you
        crazy.

Ivan Delinov

Oh, yes, I am looking for summer job,
    new one.
Do you have opportunity for me?
Last summer I work at ball park
Selling beer, pretzels, and peanuts.
It was nice to be in fresh air,
But I am loooking for new, how you say,
Higher level of celery.
Oh yes, salary, thank you.
Ah, America is fine country.
Such big distinction between
Throwing pretzels and throwing fastballs.
It bothered me that star players
Earn salary of $1,000,000 a year,
Which is about $143,000 a month for
    seven months' work,
Which is about $36,000 a week,
Which is about $5,000 a day,
While I worked for peanuts.

Arthur Gabriel

I want to ask her out,
But I'm scared silly to do it.
Roxanne is the prettiest girl I've ever seen.
What if she's already goin' out with somebody?
What if she hangs up on me?
What if she says no?
Girls have it so easy.
All they have to do is
Sit by the phone and wait.
What do you think, Mr. C.?
Should I call?
Easy for you to say.
I know it's just one date,
Maybe not very important to you,
But it means the world to me.
I am so scared that
I will never be liked.
Ever.

Roxanne DeVerona

I want him to ask me out,
But I'm scared silly he won't.
Arthur is the cutest guy I've ever seen.
What if he's already goin' out with somebody?
What if he doesn't call me on the phone?
What if he doesn't like me?
Guys have it so easy.
All they have to do is
Pick up the phone and call.
What do you think, Mr. C.?
Will he call?
Easy for you to say.
I know it's just one date,
Maybe not very important to you,
But it means the world to me.
I am so scared that
I will never be liked.
Ever.

Matthew Egan

Nice of you to look over my application, Mr. C.
You think I have enough awards? Really?
I want to impress my father that I'm
    applying there.
But you know I never seem to impress him enough.
If I get a 96 on a test,
He asks what happened to the other four points.
If I come in second in a swim meet
He wants to know why I didn't finish first.
If my board scores improve fifty points
He'll think they should have gone up a hundred.
However good I am
It's just not good enough.
Whatever heights I reach
It won't be high enough.
He just keeps raising the bar
Higher and higher.
I doubt I will ever clear it.

Frannie Byrd

Boo!
Did I scare you?
Just came back to say hello.
Been a couple of months, hasn't it?
They just gave me a day pass.
I'm OK as long as I take my medication.
You think I look all right?
Yeah? Not like the last time you saw me, huh,
When you had to call the emergency squad.
I really wasn't going to jump,
But I gotta admit
I kind of enjoyed all the attention.
I want to thank you
For being so kind to me that day,
For telling me I wasn't crazy
When I really knew I was crazy.
I'm going to make a life for myself, you'll see.
I'll get my equivalency diploma.
Can I come back to visit you?
Anytime? You mean it?
Thanks!

Mr. Royce Egan

(Matthew's father) • Telephone conversation

I just got Matthew's report card
And I'm less than thrilled about it.
A ninety average is good, you say?
Not good enough for Harvard, for Yale, for Matthew.
He certainly has the ability to do better.
I don't think he is applying himself.
Is there anything I can do to get his grades up?
What do you mean, stop pressuring him?
Listen, if I had brought home a report card
    like that
My father would have whaled me.
I remember one time
He locked me in my room all day
And refused to let me out
Till I finished studying for my chemistry final.
Then another time he . . .
Yes, I know we're talking about Matthew.
That's the point. I only want the best
    for my son.
Just like my father wanted for me.

Stanley Flowers

I have everything I want:
My own room,
My own car,
My own sound system.
I have parents who love me, most times.
A sister who's tolerable, sometimes,
A best friend who's loyal every time,
And a girl who loves me all the time.
But you want to know somethin'?
All that I got—
I don't feel I deserve it.
Not that I'm about to give anything back.
Not that I would trade places with anyone.
Yet, when it's late at night
And I am alone with the thoughts in my head,
I feel someone is going to discover my secret:
I didn't do nothin' to rate any of this.
And this someone will steal into my room
And quickly and quietly take everything away.

FRIDAY

Penny Arkanian

Last term when I had Mr. Renniker
I washed his boards,
  ran his errands,
  set up his science experiments,
  collected his lab reports,
  graded his exams,
  straightened up his desk,
  added up his attendance,
  sharpened his pencils,
  and did other things
  I'm too embarrassed to mention.
Just a few minutes ago
He passed me in the hall.
He didn't even stop and say hello.
It's like I never even existed.
I am such a fool!

Mrs. Beverly Blumenthall

(Stefan's mother) • Telephone conversation

You're right I'm upset.
What's going on in that school anyway?
He didn't have to tell me what happened.
I saw the bruises all over his face.
I don't care if it happened a block away.
The school's still responsible
As far as I'm concerned.
And why weren't the cops called?
What kind of school are you running anyway?
My Stefan is a good boy.
I've raised him to be courteous and caring.
Better I should have raised him to be a fighter.
Maybe I should take him out of your school
    altogether.
Tell me, Mr. Candler, why do children hurt
    each other?
What kind of world are we living in anyway?
I don't have any answers,
And it seems to me neither do you.
Good day, Mr. Candler. You'll be hearing from me,
Or from my lawyer.

Preston Baliss

Me and my mother had this argument.
She found this piece in my room,
A .38 I was hidin' for my man, Slick.
She lit into me,
Slapped me upside the head
And said I was nothin' but trouble.
I got outta there real fast,
Took the gun and went to find Slick.
Before I knows it
Two plainclothes dudes arrest me
And take me to Central Booking.
I spent two nights in jail before they
    let me go.
It was like a sewer, man, rats and everything.
You wanna hear the kicker?
Check this out.
My mom was the one that had me arrested.
What she go and do that for?
I was only playin'.
I wasn't gonna use the gun or nothin'.

Francisco Lopez

I walked outta Berringer's class
'Cause he never does nothin'.
He just sits at his desk
And tells us funny stories
About his wife, his kids, his car.
How are funny stories
Gonna help me find a job?
How are bad jokes about his wife
Gonna advance me in life?
The teacher I got before Berringer is worse.
Hoyt's so boring he puts *himself* to sleep.
No, I don't have a degree in teaching,
But after twelve years of education
I know a good teacher when I see one,
And it ain't them.
Both those teachers are jokes, Mr. Candler,
But I ain't laughin'.

Ellie Isaacs

Mr. Candler, what's your position on sex?
Oh, I don't mean it that way, stop laughing.
I mean, do you think my mother
Has the right to tell me what to do?
Or more exactly, what not to do?
It's my body, not her business.
My feelings, not her rules.
She reads about the rise in teenage pregnancy
And thinks I'm personally responsible
For an increased birth rate.
What with all the headlines
She believes I'll get every disease
Known to and transmitted by man,
Or more exactly, my boyfriend.
Just because I love loving
Does not make me a wicked, hateful girl.
Tell her that, will you?
I can't.
She talks to me all night long,
But she hasn't listened in years.

Anonymous Parent

Telephone conversation

No, I am not going to tell you my name.
But I know who you are.
You're the one who's listening to her lies.
What does she tell you?
That I beat her up?
That's a lie, I'm tellin' you.
Of course I'll slap her around once in a while
When she gets outta line.
But it's none of your business, got that?
No, I won't tell you my name.
You leave my daughter alone
With all that psychological garbage.
Or I'll get you.
I know where you live.

Gloria Simonetti

Mr. Candler, where are you going?
You can't go to lunch now.
You gotta help me find it.
I've looked everywhere,
My last period class, my locker, the stairs,
Even the sink in the bathroom.
I can't calm down
Until I find my "number one" charm.
It was just on my neck,
On a gold chain.
Yes, I've checked the lost and found.
They never find anything.
My grandfather gave me that charm
When I was six years old.
I've always worn it.
I never take it off.
It was the last present I got
    from my grandfather
Before he died.
Please, Mr. Candler, you just gotta help me
    find that charm.

Ramona Castillo

When the soldiers came in the middle of the night
There was no moon watching over
Our little house in Central America.
My parents hid me under the bed
And gave me a towel to chew on
So that I would not cry out.
It was the last time I saw them.
The next morning relatives found me
Still under the bed, still clutching the towel.
We waited for days, but there was no word.
Finally my relatives sent me to an uncle here,
To start a new life, to outrun the tragedy.
I did not like my new land or language.
I felt embarrassed by my own accent.
Then, about a year ago, a nice teacher,
    Mr. Loomis,
Showed me how to take photographs,
Showed me how to speak with film and f-stops.
I try to shoot many pictures of children smiling,
To capture in their bright, glowing faces
A childhood stolen from me
In the middle of a moonless night,
Five years ago in time, but
Yesterday in my heart and in my memory.

Henry (Hank) Grendell

Mr. Candler, would you say I'm too fat?
Hefty? Well, that's one way of putting it.
Occupational hazard, I guess.
I work the snack counter, fries and stuff,
Down at Bowlmore Lanes.
When my uncle Harry got me the job
I thought I was the luckiest guy alive.
I love to bowl; I love to eat.
What could be better?
I also thought I'd make some new friends.
In the beginning the job was great.
I met some terrific new people.
Then I realized they just wanted
Free food instead of free friendship.
Now the guys don't hang around the snack bar much.
They prefer to strike up conversations
With the girls hangin' around the video games.
I know now I will have plenty of time to spend
Eating—fry by fry,
Bowling—frame by frame,
Alone.

Mr. Harry Grendell

(Henry's uncle) • Telephone conversation

You don't know me, sir,
But I know all about you.
I want to thank you
For spending so much time with my nephew, Henry.
He talks about you a lot,
How you always have time for him, how you always
    listen.
Please don't say it's only your job,
    I know better.
You don't get paid extra for being nice,
For helping him with his problems.
You know my brother and sister-in-law died
    last year,
In a plane crash; it was terrible.
Henry's living with me now,
But I'm afraid I'm too old to deal with
    teenagers.
Yes, I did get him a job,
But it isn't enough.
At night I still hear him crying in his room.
There are no words to comfort his loss
And mine.
But I did want to thank you
For making his pain a little less painful.
You're a good man, sir.

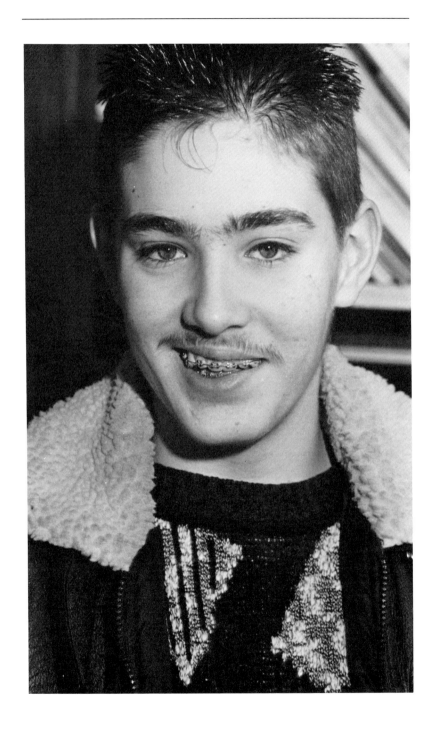

Gavin Orloff

Mr. Candler, I gotta talk to you.
Something bad happened.
You know I'm on the wrestling team, right?
Yeah, well, last period I had practice.
Something came over me.
I can't explain it; I became possessed.
I looked at Bud across the mat from me
And I knew I was going to hurt him.
I wrenched his arm.
It broke, I think.
I went for his neck
And I heard some strange noise.
And then—then I pulled his leg,
Just like I'm pulling yours.
Gotcha, Mr. Candler.
Had you goin', didn't I?
You have a good day now, you hear?

Madeline Rothstein

While my mother was trying to figure out
The right pattern for the new kitchen wallpaper,
I asked her a hypothetical question.
I said, "Mom, suppose I was goin' out
With a boy from a different neighborhood?"
"I guess he'd have to take the bus,"
    she said, smiling.
"Suppose I was goin' out
With a boy from a different religion?"
"As long as you don't convert," she said,
    slightly smiling.
"Suppose I was goin' out
With a boy from a different race?"
"Over my dead body," she said, not smiling at all.
Then she smiled again and told me to get
The other sample from the table.
How do I tell her that Ernesto,
Who wants to take me to the prom,
Who is the sweetest boy alive,
Is different on all three counts?
My mother has a sharp eye for color.
She's bound to notice that me and
    my boyfriend clash.
And she'll go right up the unfinished
    kitchen wall.

Mr. Mark Candler

Counselor

I'm beat, can't even move.
Got to get home,
Maybe catch a few winks
Before I have to
> take the car in for a muffler,
> go to the dentist at five.
> pick up supper, Chinese maybe,
> pick up Jamie from Mrs. Brenner.

My desk?
The mess can keep till Monday.
Where'd I put my keys?
They were here a second ago.

It's OK, Randy, you can come in.
You look upset.
That bad?
You better sit down.
No, I wasn't leaving,
Not just yet, that is.
So what's up?
Just tell me about it—slowly.
I'm here,
Like always.